anthony ant

and the Lost City

anthony ant

and the Lost City

STORY BY JOHN GRANT

Based on the TV series

INSPIRED BY THE BOOKS OF LORNA AND GRAHAM PHILPOT

A Dolphin ★ Paperback

First published in Great Britain in 1999
as a Dolphin Paperback
by Orion Children's Books
a division of the Orion Publishing Group Ltd
Orion House
5 Upper St Martin's Lane
London WC2H 9EA

TV series copyright © HIT Entertainment Plc and YTV co-productions 1999
Based on the books by Lorna and Graham Philpot
Illustrations by The County Studio
Illustrations copyright © Orion Children's Books 1999

A catalogue record for this book is available from the British Library.
Printed in Great Britain

"**O**uch!" cried Anthony, as he fell off his skateboard for the tenth time in only ten minutes.

Anthony, Kevin, Ruby, Alexi and Terry were on the bank of the stream, where they liked to go in the afternoons. Anthony was working hard on his double-flip wheelie. Kevin was practising his juggling, as usual.

"Whoops!" said Kevin as he dropped one of the balls. It fell to the ground, bounced once, bounced twice, and plopped

into the water. Kevin raced along the bank after it. But the current was swift, and soon the ball was only a dot in the distance.

Sadly he walked back to rejoin the rest of the gang.

"What are you all talking about?" asked Kevin.

"Alexi says my family are special," said

Ruby. "It seems us red ants are pretty rare, and in the old days we were top of the heap. But I'm not interested in all that stuff. I don't think it matters who you are."

"Boring!" said Kevin. "I wish I hadn't lost that ball. It's not the same juggling with only two."

"Let's go and find it," said Anthony.

"It will be no good," said Kevin. "The current's too fast. I tried."

"We'll go by water," said Anthony. "And here comes our transport!"

A long, slim, flat piece of wood was drifting towards them. It was a Bigfoot lolly stick!

"Grab it, Terry," said Anthony. "We'll soon have your ball, Kevin."

Terry leaned out and grabbed the stick as it came close to the bank, and held it steady. "All aboard!" he cried.

"Cool," said Kevin, jumping quickly on to the stick.

"Drifting along with the stream – how romantic!" said Ruby, clutching Kevin and jumping on behind him.

"I'll probably regret this," said Alexi with a sigh. All the same, she took a firm grip on her spectacles and sprang aboard.

Anthony followed, his skateboard tucked firmly under his arm. Terry scrambled on to the stick and pushed off.

"Wait for me! Wait for me!" Billy and Aphido came running along the bank. With a wild leap they tumbled aboard as the stick moved out into midstream.

The stream wound this way and that. The stick rocked in the choppy stretches and drifted slowly where the water was calm. Then, from ahead, there came a hissing, gurgling sound. The stream began to flow faster and faster towards a round pool. As the water began to flow round in circles the stick was swept round too, towards the centre, where the water rushed down and vanished into a dark hole. The stick flipped up and then twisted and twirled down, down into the dark.

The twisting and twirling stopped.

There was not a glimmer of light. The gang clung tightly to the stick. Was this the centre of the earth? Once or twice they caught a blink of light high above them. There was a glint of daylight and the stick and its passengers shot out of a stone arch on the crest of a foaming torrent. The stick bucked and reared. The gang clung on with all their hands. Anthony looked round. At least they were still all aboard.

There was a loud cry: "YEEE!"

It was Kevin, laughing and shouting as the stick bounced and slid over and through the rushing water.

"I don't believe it," cried Anthony, "He actually likes it!"

One bank was almost out of sight.

"This isn't our stream," said Terry. "Where are we?"

The stick drifted close to the nearer side. Then, from overhead, there came a loud droning noise. The gang looked up to see a group of large winged creatures cruising above them in formation. Then, without warning, they peeled off into a dive and zoomed past just above head level.

"Dragonflies!" cried Ruby. "Perhaps they've never seen ants before. Here they come again. For another look!"

This time the dragonflies were so close that the gang had to cling hard not to be

blown off the stick. The gang was under observation! There was an ant mounted on each dragonfly. A red ant!

"I have a nasty feeling that we may be trespassing," said Kevin. "That was no welcoming party."

The stick had drifted close to the shore. It came to rest on a little patch of sand.

"All ashore who's going ashore!" cried Anthony, tucking his skateboard under his arm. One by one they jumped on to the sand. Beyond the sand there was scrubby grass and some leafy plants. Terry went to have a closer look.

Kevin looked back across the stream. A few leaves and twigs floated by on the current, but he still couldn't see any sign of his juggling ball.

two

"There's a sort of rough track over here," yelled Terry. "And I'm sure I can see footprints."

"What kind of footprints?" Anthony called back.

"Ant footprints."

"Then let's follow them," said Anthony, and he led the way.

The trail was in deep shadow in places. Odd sounds and strange rustlings could be heard on every side. In a clearing, huge fearsome creatures grazed among the stems of grass.

"What are those horrible great things?" whispered Ruby.

"Stag beetles," Anthony whispered. "Shh, be careful not to disturb them. They could be dangerous."

They crept through the grass trying not to be noticed.

"Listen! I can hear voices," said Kevin.

"And footsteps," whispered Alexi. "Marching footsteps."

A long line of soldier ants came into view, marching three abreast, with their leader in the front.

"Wow!" breathed Ruby. "They're red ants, like me. I've never seen so many. I wonder where they come from?"

The line of ants came to a halt, right in front of the gang. The leader stepped forward and saluted.

"Greetings," he said. "I have orders to take you to the City."

"What City?" said Kevin.

"Whose orders?" said Anthony.

But before they could say anything else the red ants surrounded them, and Anthony, Terry, Ruby, Alexi, Kevin, Billy and Aphido found themselves in the middle of a column of soldier ants. There was no sound from the red ants, only the tramp, tramp of hundreds of marching feet. The

gang kept close to each other and did their
best to keep up with the soldiers.

Soon the rough track joined a broad,
paved road. Just the thing for a skateboard,
thought Anthony. On either side of the
road stood huge statues of ants, chipped and
broken, and covered with moss and lichen.

The road led through a great gate in a mighty wall, as overgrown and ruined as the statues. Beyond the gate was a city.

"This must be the lost City of the Red Ants!" gasped Alexi. "I always thought it was just a legend."

The red ants marched them across a broad square. Important-looking buildings stood all round it, but they were half-ruined. No ants were going in and out of them. No ants appeared in the square to see the gang's arrival.

"I wonder where everyone is?" thought Anthony. He felt a bit scared.

Just then the leader of the soldier ants shouted, "Halt!" and the column stopped in front of a crumbling archway. Out from the archway came a red ant wearing a splendid uniform.

"The Mighty Rubrica welcomes you to her palace," said the red ant, bowing low to each of the gang in turn. "Come with me and I will take you to her."

The gang followed the red ant through the arch, along a corridor, up one flight of stairs and down another, until at last they came to a large beautifully carved door.

"Scary!" whispered Alexi. "What do you think we do now?"

The red ant flung open the door and called out, "Enter the presence of the Mighty Rubrica, Ruler of the Red Ants!"

"That's what we do," said Anthony. "Come on, gang. Follow the red carpet."

At the far end of the red carpet there was a glittering figure sitting on a glittering throne. On each side stood crowds of red ants, and in front of them the soldiers who had been their escort made a guard of honour. A fanfare of trumpets sounded. Anthony led the way towards the throne.

The Mighty Rubrica rose and held out all her arms in greeting.

"Welcome!" she cried. "We have long awaited your coming!"

Anthony was about to say something in

reply, but the Mighty Rubrica was
beckoning to Ruby. She stepped forward
nervously. Should she bow? Or curtsey?
But it was the Mighty Rubrica who bowed.
To Ruby. She turned to the crowd.

"This is the day we have longed for," she cried in a loud voice. "The Empire of the Red Ants will rise again. The Spirit of Rubra, the Blessed Princess, has come among us at last!"

"What's she talking about?" whispered Anthony to the others.

"Dunno," Kevin whispered back, "but this Rubrica is cool!"

"It's an ancient legend," whispered Alexi. "A prophecy. The Empire of the Red Ants will become great again with the coming of a Blessed Princess. But she has been dead for centuries!"

"And they think Ruby is her ghost or something?" asked Anthony.

"That's about it, I should think," said Kevin. "In my opinion, our friend Ruby is Number One here."

The Mighty Rubrica took one of Ruby's hands in hers. She led her forward to face the crowd. "Speak to your people," she said. "Tell them you bring hope to the land of the red ants."

Ruby cleared her throat and bawled, "Hi, you red ants! I bring hope to your land."

Everyone cheered. The trumpets blew

another fanfare. And the Mighty Rubrica led Ruby, the Spirit of the Blessed Princess, and the rest of the gang along the red carpet and out of the throne room.

three

"**T**hank you very much, Ruby," said the Mighty Rubrica. "That was quite a performance. The people loved it."

"You mean it isn't true, the Blessed Princess bit?" said Ruby.

"It's as true as any legend ever is," said the Mighty Rubrica. "The red ants were a great people in their day."

"They were terrible!" exclaimed Alexi. "They made slaves of the other ants. That's how they managed to build the City."

"I know, I know," said the Mighty Rubrica. "My ancestor, Rubrica the First, was cruel and ambitious. But I'm not like that. I just want my people to be happy, and they are happy now they believe the Blessed Princess has returned."

"Tell me," said Anthony, "how did you know we were coming?"

"Easy," said the Mighty Rubrica. "Border patrol. The dragonflies are very useful. And it gives them a chance to show off their aerobatics. They reported that a group of young ants was coming this way, and that one of them was a red ant. We don't often get to see other ants, you know."

"Cool!" said Kevin.

"Now, let me show you the City, or what's left of it," said the Mighty Rubrica. "This is where your ancestors came from, isn't it, Ruby?"

"I Dunno," said Ruby. "My ma and pa came to Antville when I was just a grub." The Mighty Rubrica led the way out into the streets of the City. Anthony and the gang just stared around them, amazed. Everything was built of stones – and what stones! Ants are strong but the gang couldn't imagine how they had managed to move stones of this size.

The City was bigger than Antville, but

most of it seemed to be in ruins. Many of the stones had fallen over and were covered with moss, but you could still see the carvings on them.

"Those carvings were done when we red ants were so powerful that all the other ants trembled at our name," said the Mighty Rubrica. "Especially at the name of Rubrica the First. But long ago, Bigfoot passed this way and trod on a stone with Rubrica's image carved on it. It fell over, and from that day on, things have gone badly for us. Our empire has shrunk to just a ruined city. We have lost the skills to rebuild it. We live below ground, instead of in our grand houses."

"Isn't there anything you can do?" asked Alexi.

"Not unless we can get the fallen image of Rubrica the First to stand upright. Only

then will we have good fortune again. But now that the Blessed Princess has come, my people really believe that everything will come right."

"Where is this fallen image?" asked Anthony. "Perhaps Terry could lift it. He's very strong."

"It would take more than strength," said the Mighty Rubrica. "The ants who first raised it were very clever. They did it with ropes and poles, but we don't know how."

"Ropes and poles?" said Ruby. "I've watched my Uncle Derrick moving rocks with a rope and pole rig. What do you say, Terry? You've got the muscle. I've got the know-how. Some of it, anyway. Let's try. And that's the Blessed Princess speaking."

"I'll take you there," said the Mighty

Rubrica. She led the way into the tall grass. There were more ruins, and heaps of broken stone to climb over. There was damp moss everywhere. It squelched underfoot and made green stains on hands and clothes.

"And they say a rolling stone gathers no moss," panted Kevin. "They want to try rolling one here. Yuk!"

"This was a very important part of the City in its day," said the Mighty Rubrica. "Every ant who was any ant lived here. Somewhere round here was a noble square, and in the middle they set up the great stone with the image of Rubrica the First."

The going was rough. Billy, with Aphido snuffling at his heels, was able to wriggle and squeeze through the spaces between the stones. But the others needed every hand and foot available to an ant to slither and scramble over damp stone and wet moss.

"I've got to have a rest!" said Alexi. She sat down on a flat, sloping stone. She started picking away at the moss. A carved stone eye looked up at her.

"Hey, I think I'm sitting on Rubrica the First!" cried Alexi.

The Mighty Rubrica came over to have a look, and peeled off some more moss. Now, two ferocious eyes stared up at them.

"She's watching us," whispered Anthony. "I saw the eyes move!"

"Me too," said Ruby. "I'm sure she blinked." And she huddled closer to Alexi.

"Trick of the light!" scoffed Alexi. At that moment a chill gust of wind rustled the grass stems.

"I don't think she appreciates our crawling all over her," laughed Kevin.

But no one else laughed. There was a creepy feeling in the air.

"There's something else," said Alexi. "Ancient writing. Like I've seen in the museum. I wish I could read it."

They started to clean off the moss. A face appeared, its mouth twisted in an evil snarl. Rubrica the First was a terrifying sight. It was hard not to look at her. When Ruby called out, "The stone's sunk right into the ground," the gang gladly tore themselves away from the image and joined her in the mud and dirt.

"It will need digging out. And lifting," said Terry.

"That can be arranged," said the Mighty Rubrica. "If the Blessed Princess asks for help, the people won't refuse. Tonight you are my guests at a special banquet, and we will make an announcement then."

The banquet was splendid. The gang had never tasted such delicious honeydew. And after the banquet there was some entertainment. The band played. Dancers danced. Acrobats leaped and tumbled. There were jugglers so skilful that Kevin almost decided to give up trying. And singers sang sad songs about the Good Old Days.

"They were only good for some of the ants," muttered Alexi.

When the last of the jugglers and singers and dancers and acrobats had finished, everyone turned to look at the gang.

"What are they all staring at?" whispered Alexi.

The Mighty Rubrica said, "It is one of our red ant customs for the guests to provide some little entertainment. Would one of you, perhaps –?"

Anthony, Terry, Kevin, Billy, Aphido and Alexi all looked at each other. Then they all looked at Ruby.

"Go on, Ruby," said Anthony. "You're the only one who can sing."

So Ruby stood up.

"I'll sing you a song my grandpa taught me," said Ruby. "He used to herd aphids."

And Ruby, accompanied by the band, sang:

"A six-legged friend,

A six-legged friend,

He'll never let you down.

He's honest and faithful up to the end.

That wonderful two - four - six —

Six-legged friend."

By the third verse the company was joining in the chorus. Ruby finished her song to wild applause.

"Thanks, everyone," said Ruby when the applause had died down. "And now, I have got something to say. I need your help."

She explained about the fallen image. Then Terry stood up and said it would need the help and strength of every able-bodied ant in the City to set it up again.

"Yes! Yes! We'll do it!" cried all of the red ants, shouting and waving their arms.

"We will spread the word! Tomorrow we will raise Rubrica the First! Three cheers for the Blessed Princess!"

Next morning Athony led the gang back to the fallen image. The Mighty Rubrica stayed behind. She said she had some important and urgent ruling to do.

Crowds of red ants were already marching in the same direction, carrying picks and shovels. A team of harvester ants carried scythes, machetes and billhooks. There were ants in teams hauling long, stout poles and coils of strong rope.

When they reached the fallen stone,

Anthony clambered up on the head of Rubrica the First and spoke to the crowds.

"Today's the day the image of Rubrica the First will rise again! Her spirit will be made happy and you and your City will flourish once more!"

The crowds cheered. Terry jumped up. "In Antville we work in teams. Each for all and all for each. You know what you've got to do. Let's go!"

And they did! The harvesters chopped at the tall grass stems to make a wide clearing around the stone. Then ants with picks and shovels dug away soil and roots from the sides.

Ruby went from team to team. The red ants seemed to work harder when she passed. And they worked harder still when she spoke to them.

"This is crazy," she said to herself. "They treat me like a real princess. If only they knew! It's me. Ruby Red Ant. Now, if it was Alexi – she knows about legends and lots of stuff like that. I don't really understand any of it."

Anthony was looking up at the tallest grass stems as they waved to and fro in the breeze. There were red ants clinging to the tips. "What are those ants doing up there?" Anthony asked a passing ant.

"Lookouts," said the ant. "They're looking out for rhinoceros beetles."

Alexi was crouched low in the mud close to the stone, staring at the ancient writing on it. "If only I could read it!" she said to herself.

"Below there!" One of the lookouts was waving his arms.

"What is it?" Anthony called.

"Rhinoceros beetles! A whole herd! Coming this way!"

Before the lookout had even finished speaking, the red ants disappeared. The gang were on their own. Aphido was tense, sniffing the breeze. A faint rustling came from the long grass. The gang dived beneath some tumbled stone slabs where the grass still stood high enough for them to hide behind. They peered through the stems. The sounds were getting close.

Alexi gasped. Terry gulped. For once, Kevin had nothing to say. Ruby just stared in wonder. Billy tried to make himself smaller than he already was by crouching behind a broad grass blade.

The leader of the herd of giant beetles shouldered its way menacingly between the grasses. Its long, sharp horns caught the light, and its body armour gleamed sinister and black. It paused, sensing the presence of the ants. It looked one way, then the other, but it was too short-sighted to be able to see them.

At last the beetle moved on, followed by a dozen more. The gang crawled out from cover. The red ants reappeared and set to work as if nothing had happened.

Anthony asked one of the harvester ants, "Do rhinoceros beetles eat ants?"

"Nobody knows," said the red ant.

"Why not?" asked Anthony.

"Because," said the ant, "nobody has been stupid enough to stay around to find out. That's why not. OK?"

By noon all the earth and roots and

stones had been dug away from around the fallen stone. It was clear of moss. It looked just as it had the day Bigfoot trod on it.

The workers stopped to eat.

Before work started again, Ruby found a piece of soft stone. On one of the flat blocks she cleared a space in the moss and began to draw a diagram. "Hope they all understand it," she said. "I'm not sure I do. I wish Uncle Derrick was here."

Anthony watched her. "You're good at gadgets, Ruby," he said.

"This isn't a gadget," said Ruby. "This is serious engineering. I've seen my uncle lift some funny things with poles and ropes, but never a fallen image. I just hope it works, that's all!"

"We'll soon know," said Anthony. "Time to get started."

Everyone had finished eating. "Gather round!" called Terry.

He explained what each had to do. Ruby pointed to the diagram she had drawn on the stone and explained how the poles and ropes would help to lift Rubrica the First again.

"OK, let's do it," cried Terry, and every ant went to his place.

Poles were placed in position. Ants dug and crawled under the image, dragging

ropes. Soon, Rubrica the First was held in a web of stout poles and strong ropes. Ruby checked everything was in its place. Terry checked that the many knots were secure. Then he stood back. He spat on his hands and grabbed a rope. The other members of the gang grabbed a rope each.

"One! Two! Heave!" shouted Terry.

They all heaved. Ropes groaned. Poles creaked. And nothing happened. Another heave – and the stone moved ever so slightly and bumped back again.

Terry made one or two adjustments.

"Right," he shouted. "Again, heave!"

Again the stone moved. Then, with a loud sucking sound, it lifted very slowly out of the mud. The red ants with the poles ran to push them into place under the stone to take the weight.

"Again, heave!" shouted Terry.

Bit by bit the stone image of Rubrica the First began to rise. Mud and dirt dropped from it. It was almost there, but the red ants were exhausted. It needed one last effort. Poles were placed to take the weight again. Terry and Ruby examined the lifting rig and adjusted it.

Then, "One last heave!" shouted Terry.

And the great stone stood upright

But only for a moment. It was toppling forward! Red ants scattered in panic. Terry grabbed armfuls of ropes, took a deep breath and pulled. Rubrica the First rocked back and then stood still. Her evil face looked down on her people as it used to do.

For a moment the red ants backed off . They were a bit frightened.

Then someone started to cheer. The cheering swelled until it carried all the way to the City and the ants who lived below it. Old ants and children came running to see the image. It was standing upright at last. Did that mean the good times of old would return to the city?

The Mighty Rubrica herself appeared.

"What an ugly old ant my ancestor was!" she said. "But well done, everyone. Perhaps when she's been cleaned up she'll be nicer looking."

five

When everything was over, Anthony and the rest of the gang made their way back to the City.

"Rubrica the First looked a bit sad and lost, didn't she?" said Ruby.

"She was evil!" said Alexi.

"Maybe she was, but she used to stand in a noble square. Why don't we bring her back to the City Square?" said Anthony.

The gang thought that was a great idea.

"Let's go and tell the Mighty Rubrica,"

said Ruby. So off they went to the palace.

The Mighty Rubrica said she had been thinking the same thing.

"But how do we get her there?" she asked. "My ancestors must have moved her, but no one knows how they did it."

"It shouldn't be too hard," said Anthony. "Collect all the wagons in town —"

"Wagons? What's a wagon?" asked the Mighty Rubrica.

"A wagon? Oh, er, sort of like a big handcart," said Anthony.

"And what's a handcart?" asked the Mighty Rubrica with a frown.

Anthony laughed. "You're joking! A handcart is a sort of box on wheels that you —"

"Wheels? What are they?" asked the Mighty Rubrica, in a very puzzled voice.

Anthony looked round at the others. He couldn't believe his ears.

"This is totally uncool!" said Kevin. "You lot are really in the dark!"

"Well, how do you move heavy loads?" asked Anthony.

"Oh, we haul them on sleds," said the Mighty Rubrica. "Or else we carry them slung on poles."

"No kidding?" said Kevin.

"No kidding. But you still haven't told me what wheels are."

"Wait here," said Anthony.

"Of course you can't know what wheels are," said Alexi. "You didn't need wheels in the old days. You had slaves to do all the lifting and carrying."

Anthony returned. He held something

hidden behind his back. He nodded to a heavy marble urn on a pedestal.

"See that urn? Put it on the floor," he said to Terry.

"Try pushing it," he said to the Mighty Rubrica. The Mighty Rubrica could barely move the urn.

Anthony brought out his skateboard and placed it on the floor. He nodded to Terry. Terry lifted the enormous urn on to the board.

"Now try to push it," he said to the Mighty Rubrica. With a gentle push, the Mighty Rubrica sent the skateboard and the urn trundling across the floor. "It's magic!" she exclaimed.

"Wheels," said Anthony. "Round things on axles. And very useful, too."

"Rubrica the First will be brought into the City on wheels," cried the Mighty

Rubrica. She ordered the royal carpenters and blacksmiths to make a giant copy of Anthony's skateboard.

Anthony explained that there was still a problem. Wheels needed paved roads, but the statue of Rubrica the First stood in a mess of mud and trampled grass.

"There were paved roads there in the old

days," said the Mighty Rubrica. "All we have to do is find them."

Squads of red ants armed with spades went to work. And sure enough, under all the dirt, there were smooth paving stones. They had soon uncovered a broad highway leading straight into the City Square.

At last everything was ready. With the aid of more poles and ropes, Rubrica the

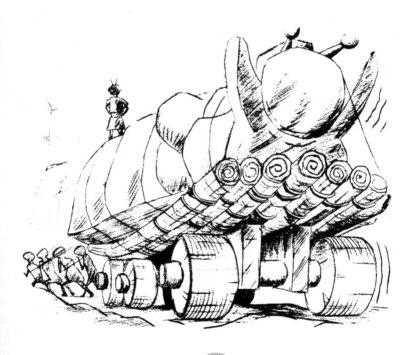

First was lifted on to her carriage. More ropes held her securely in place. Crowds of red ants were already lining the route. Everything was ready for the journey. The Mighty Rubrica herself would lead the way.

At the last moment the Mighty Rubrica called to Anthony, who stood close by, "Without your help none of this could have been done. You shall lead the procession!"

Teams of red ants pulled and pushed. Slowly the wheels began to turn. The red ants lining the road gasped in wonder. Those ants farther away heard the distant rumble of the wheels.

Then they finally saw the towering figure of Rubrica the First. The Mighty Rubrica marched in front of her ancestor, and in front of her came Ruby, the Blessed Princess, and her companions Alexi, Kevin, Terry and Billy, with Aphido trotting proudly at her heels. Leading the whole company, though, was Anthony Ant – on his skateboard!

There was another great feast that night. There were many speeches by important red ants. They said good times were coming to their land. Wonderful things would be done using wheels. They would move rocks. They would move mountains!

The Mighty Rubrica rose and proposed a toast to the gang.

"To Terry, Alexi, Kevin and Billy. To Ruby, the spirit of the Blessed Princess. And to Anthony, who showed us all the miracle of the wheel. They came bravely from their world into ours. We will always remember them. We wish them all a long life and lots of happiness!"

And that was really the end of the story. The Mighty Rubrica arranged for the gang to be flown home to Antville by dragonfly. One for Anthony, Alexi, Ruby, Kevin, Billy and Aphido. And an extra-strong one to carry Terry.

Kevin wanted to travel home by water. Anthony pointed out that things did not usually float upstream. If they did, Kevin's juggling ball might just be waiting for him when he got home to Antville.

One day, the gang were sitting in the Clubhouse chatting about this and that. "What do you think the red ants have used the wheel for?" asked Terry.

"Water mills," said Ruby.

"Revolving bookcases," said Alexi.

"Exercise bicycles," said Terry.

"Aphid-drawn carriages," said Anthony.

"Well, I've been thinking," said Kevin. "What did those red ants think was super cool? What really grabbed them?"

"What?" asked the gang.

"In my opinion, right now every red ant in the City is whizzing around on their own skateboards!"

And Kevin was probably right!